PEOPLE IN MY FAMILY

by Jeffrey Moss • illustrated by Carol Nicklaus

Based on the song, "FIVE PEOPLE IN MY FAMILY"
© Festival Attractions, Inc. 1969, music and lyrics by Jeffrey Moss

Featuring Jim Henson's Sesame Street Muppets

A SESAME STREET/GOLDEN PRESS BOOK
Published by Western Publishing Company, Inc. in conjunction with Children's Television Workshop.

© 1983, 1971 Children's Television Workshop. Sesame Street Muppets © Muppets, Inc. 1983. All rights reserved. Printed in the U.S.A. No part of this book may be reproduced or copied in any form without written permission from the publisher. Sesame Street® and the Sesame Street sign are trademarks and service marks of Children's Television Workshop. GOLDEN®, GOLDEN & DESIGN®, GOLDEN PRESS®, and A GOLDEN SUPER SHAPE BOOK are trademarks of Western Publishing Company, Inc. ISBN: 0-307-10070-7/ISBN: 0-307-68995-6 (lib. bdg.) A B C D E F G H I J

I've got five people in my family,
And those five people make me glad.

There's a sister

and two brothers.

And a mother

and a dad.

Five is such a pretty number.
I'm awfully glad that I've
Five people in my family.
1 2 3 4 5

I've got five monsters in my family,
And we all have lots of fun.

Furry wife

and scary husband.

Fuzzy daughters,

hairy son.

Five is such a scary number.
Oh, I'm so glad that I've
Five monsters in my family.
1   2   3   4   5

I've got five fingers on my left hand,
I've got five fingers on my right.

Five fingers help me wave good morning,

Help me brush my teeth at night.

Five is such a pretty number.
I'm awfully glad that I've
Five fingers on each hand.
1 2 3 4 5

Oh, five is such a pretty number.
I'm awfully glad that I've
Five people in my family.
1 2 3 4 5

1 2 3 4 5 6 7 8 9 10